JANE AUSTEN

Children's Stories

Dados Internacionais de Catalogação na Publicação (CIP) de acordo com ISBD

A933e Austen, Jane
Emma / Jane Austen. – Jandira : W. Books, 2025.
96 p. ; 12,8cm x 19,8cm. – (Jane Austen Children's Stories).

ISBN: 978-65-5294-187-9

1. Literatura infantojuvenil. 2. Romance. 3. Literatura estrangeira. 4. Literatura inglesa. 5. Amor. 6. Preconceito. 7. Inglaterra. I. Título. II. Série.

2025-589 CDD 028.5
CDU 82-93

Elaborado por Vagner Rodolfo da Silva - CRB-8/9410
Índice para catálogo sistemático:
1. Literatura infantojuvenil 028.5
2. Literatura infantojuvenil 82-93

1st edition in 2025
www.cirandacultural.com.br

JANE AUSTEN

Emma

W. Books

Chapter 1

Emma Woodhouse had everything a young woman could wish for. She lived with her father in a beautiful house called Hartfield, in a pretty town called Highbury. In fact Emma's life was so perfect, she was sometimes a little bored.

When Emma was a little girl, her favourite thing to do was pair up her dolls and hold magnificent weddings for them. As an adult, weddings were still her favourite thing. Now, however, the dolls had been replaced with real people.

Thanks to Emma's matchmaking, her sister was now happily married to Mr John Knightley. Now Emma was looking to make her next match. She decided to find a husband for her governess, Miss Taylor. Emma did not need a governess to look after her anymore, and Emma had found the perfect husband for Miss Taylor. It was their family friend Mr Weston.

It is here that we begin our story: at Miss Taylor and Mr Weston's wedding. As well as Emma, plenty of Highbury residents were at the happy event.

Miss Taylor/Mrs Weston

The new Mrs Weston had been Emma's governess for sixteen years. She had cared for her since the death of Emma's mother and they had been close friends ever since.

Mr Weston

Mr Weston had lived alone for many years since the death of his first wife. His son, Frank, lived with Mr Weston's sister-in-law, Mrs Churchill. It was decided early on that Mr Weston could

not raise a child alone, although he always felt this was a bit unfair.

Mr Woodhouse

Emma's father was a kind man with a habit of worrying about everything from the cold to the state of the roads. He especially worried about people getting married all the time.

Mr George Knightley

George Knightley was the brother of John Knightley and a great friend of Emma and Mr Woodhouse.

He had known Emma since she was little, and often walked to Hartfield from his own house, Donwell.

Miss Bates

Miss Bates was a talkative lady who had never married and lived in a small house in town. She loved sharing the weekly letters she received from her niece, Jane Fairfax, with Emma. Emma did not enjoy this.

Mr Elton

Mr Elton was the young clergyman who led Miss Taylor and Mr Weston's wedding. He was always

keen to mix with Highbury society, and accepted any invitation to do so.

As much as Emma congratulated herself on her success as a matchmaker, she felt lonely after the wedding. She would miss having Miss Taylor – no, *Mrs Weston* to keep her company. However, it was not in Emma's nature to stay sad. She would just have to find herself a *new* companion …

Chapter 2

Harriet Smith lived at the local boarding school. She was thrilled when the famous Emma Woodhouse wanted to be friends with her. Once introduced, the two quickly became very close. So much so that when Mr George Knightley came to Hartfield to return a book, he said, 'I hear you have become quite friendly with Miss Smith.'

He had found Emma in the garden, adjusting a blanket around

her father's knees despite the warm weather.

'Yes,' Emma replied. 'I think she will fit perfectly in our group of friends.'

Mr Knightley frowned and accepted a cup of tea. 'You must not force her to mix with high society,' he said. 'She is not used to it and she may feel uncomfortable.'

Emma shifted in her seat. She did not like being told what to do, especially when there was a chance that the other person was right. Luckily the only person who ever really questioned Emma's plans was Mr Knightley.

‘I understand your concern,’ replied Emma. ‘She just needs to be introduced to the right people, that’s all.’

In truth, Emma had already hatched her next matchmaking plan. She was confident this plan would work out just as well as the others.

'Mr Elton?' said Harriet, one afternoon. She and Emma were painting roses in the garden at Hartfield. Emma had just told Harriet that Mr Elton was coming for tea.

'Why yes,' replied Emma, dabbing her canvas with small, delicate strokes. 'He was most keen to come when he found out that *you* would be here.'

'M-me?' said Harriet, blushing a little.

Emma was prevented from saying anything else by the arrival of Mr Elton himself.

'What lovely paintings!' cried Mr Elton, looking over their shoulders. 'Miss Woodhouse you have a true

talent, and Miss Smith …' For a moment, the polite Mr Elton was lost for words. 'Well, your choice of colours is very nice.'

When the paintings were finished, the three companions sat together to admire them.

'Miss Smith's composition is very pretty. Do you not think, Mr Elton?' said Emma.

'It is!' agreed Mr Elton, enthusiastically. 'So pretty it should be framed.'

'Oh, I agree!' said Emma. 'Perhaps you could find a frame fine enough to suit it, Mr Elton.'

Mr Elton agreed and took Harriet's canvas with him when he left.

'Now then,' said Emma to Harriet, clasping her hands. 'What do you think? Only a man who admired a lady *very* much would take it upon himself to have her painting framed!'

Harriet looked a little unsure. 'Are you certain?' she asked. 'I could never believe a man as important as Mr Elton would consider me!'

However, Emma Woodhouse had made her mind up about the match. That, as always, was that.

Chapter 3

'He has proposed!' cried Harriet Smith only a few weeks later.

Harriet was carrying a letter, which had clearly been read many times. Her face was pink with excitement.

'Mr Elton has proposed already? How wonderful!' Emma said, taking the letter from Harriet's grasp.

Harriet shook her head. 'Not Mr Elton,' she replied. 'My friend, Robert Martin.'

Emma was shocked. She knew that Harriet was friends with a pair of sisters from a farming family called the Martins. She'd had no idea that the brother was so attached to Harriet.

'Oh,' Emma replied, 'I see ...'

Harriet's face turned from joy to confusion. She so wanted her friend to approve the match. Emma's opinion meant a lot to her.

'What have you answered?' Emma asked.

‘I haven’t yet. What do you think I should do?’ Harriet replied.

Emma linked her arm through her friend’s and they fell into step together. ‘My dear Harriet, it is not for *me* to tell you how to feel,’ she began. ‘Do you love him?’

Harriet paused. ‘I admire him …’ she began, uncertain what to say – or what her

friend would like to hear. 'And he wants to marry me.'

'You should not marry someone just because they have asked you to!' Emma laughed.

Harriet laughed too. 'No, I suppose not ...'

In the end, with a little (or a lot of) help, Harriet Smith decided *not* to marry Robert Martin. Harriet went to bed that night still confused about how she had gone from feeling such joy at the proposal to refusing it in such a short time.

Chapter 4

It was Christmas at Highbury. Mr and Mrs Weston invited their friends to a Christmas Eve dinner. After some persuasion, Mr Woodhouse decided to brave the snow and join his daughter for the event. He stayed near the window to keep an eye on the weather, just in case.

Mr Knightley and Mr Elton were also at the dinner. Mr Elton looked disappointed when Mr Knightley took the seat next to Emma at the dining table.

'Are you having a good Christmas, Mr Knightley?' Emma asked.

'Yes, although the same can't be said for one of my farmers,' Mr Knightley replied.

Emma flushed a little. 'Oh?'

'Yes. Robert Martin. He wanted to marry your friend Harriet.' Mr Knightley shook his head. 'I can't think why she would turn him down.'

Emma took a sip of her drink. 'Perhaps she feels she is too good for him,' Emma replied. 'She could marry someone better. A clergyman, perhaps?'

Mr Knightley looked at Emma for some time, slowly realising what she had done. 'Emma, have you been meddling?'

Emma shook her head so hard that the ribbons woven into her hair brushed her face. 'I merely pointed out that she could do better than Robert Martin.'

Mr Knightley was frustrated. Robert Martin had money, a farm and was a kind-hearted man. What more could a poor girl with no family like Harriet Smith hope for? He was about to say so when Mr Woodhouse rose from his chair by the window.

'The snow!' he cried. 'It is getting heavier. I am afraid we should all leave at once in case the roads get blocked.'

Although Mr Woodhouse was prone to worry, the rest of the party

agreed that an early night might be the best plan – unless they all wanted to spend Christmas Day at the Westons'. Carriages were ordered, cloaks and hats were put on, and the group hurried out into the night air.

Mr Knightley offered to take Mr Woodhouse in his carriage, which was quick and comfortable. This left Emma to ride home alone with Mr Elton.

Mr Elton climbed into the carriage and took his seat next to Emma. Emma realised he was sitting very close to her.

'My dear Miss Woodhouse,' he began. His voice was as serious as it was in church on Sundays. 'I am so glad to have this moment alone with you. You cannot be surprised to hear that I wish you to be my wife.'

Emma jumped into the opposite seat. 'Mr Elton! I *am* surprised, indeed! It is not me you like, it is Miss Smith!'

'Miss Smith?' Mr Elton frowned. 'Why on earth would you think that?'

Emma felt a flush of anger crawl up her neck. 'Because you paid so much attention to her! You complimented her *and* had her picture framed!'

Mr Elton nodded. 'I did,' he replied, reaching for Emma's hand. 'As a favour to *you*. I would do anything for you, Miss Woodhouse. Please make me the happiest man alive and agree to marry me!'

Emma snatched her hand away and tried to make herself as small as she could in the corner of the carriage. 'I am sorry for the misunderstanding,' Emma said. 'However I have no intention of marrying *anyone*.'

The carriage ride back to Hartfield was silent, and colder than the snowfall outside. Emma began to think with dread about how she was going to break the news to Harriet.

Chapter 5

Emma had days to think about how to tell Harriet what had happened. She was glad when Mr Elton took a trip to Bath and spared herself or Harriet the chance of seeing him for a while.

Harriet cried into her handkerchief on hearing that Mr Elton did not like her after all.

'Of course …' she began, between sniffs. 'It is no … wonder …

that he likes … *you* … above *me*. I was being … s-silly.'

'No!' cried Emma. 'It was my fault. I am usually a good judge of character, but Mr Elton has totally deceived me.'

Emma felt terrible as she wandered through Highbury on her way back from Harriet's boarding school. As she passed Miss Bates's cottage, she lowered her bonnet, hoping not to be seen. Unfortunately, Miss Bates's watchful eye had spotted her.

'Miss Woodhouse! Oh, Miss Woodhouse! You must come in. We have the most wonderful news!'

Emma sighed. It was probably another letter from Jane Fairfax. Emma had spent a good deal of her life smiling and nodding politely as Miss Bates read out letters from her niece. However, as she opened the door to the small parlour of Miss Bates's house, she did not find a letter – but Jane Fairfax herself!

'Now you see!' said Miss Bates, smiling. 'Our dear Jane has come to visit us. Doesn't she look well, Miss Woodhouse? Of course, you haven't seen her for many years, but trust me, Miss Woodhouse, our Jane looks most splendid this afternoon.'

While Miss Bates stopped to breathe, Emma took the opportunity of talking to Jane herself. 'It is lovely to see you,' said Emma. 'How long do you plan on staying in Highbury?'

Jane opened her mouth to speak, but it was Miss Bates's voice that answered. 'Oh, Jane will stay at least a month before she leaves to become a governess. Aren't we lucky? She can thrill us all with her excellent piano playing and sweet singing and ...'

When at last Emma made her excuses and left the cottage, she could

still hear Miss Bates's voice ringing in her ears. Emma tried to remember if Jane had spoken a single word. All Emma wished to do after her difficult morning was go to her room and lie down. However, when she reached Hartfield she noticed that Mr and Mrs Weston's carriage was outside.

‘Emma!’ cried Mrs Weston as she came to greet her on the front steps of the house. ‘We have a visitor. Frank Churchill, Mr Weston’s son, has come to visit us at last!’

Emma touched her hair and smoothed her dress before entering. She had heard of Mr Weston’s son so often she felt as though she already knew him. He was handsome, well dressed and about Emma’s age. He smiled warmly when they were introduced, and took Emma’s hand.

‘At last! The famous Miss Woodhouse!’ he said.

Chapter 6

Frank Churchill and Emma soon became firm friends. It helped that Frank wasted no time in praising Mrs Weston. Anyone who liked Mrs Weston had good sense according to Emma.

Emma and Frank got along so well, that they decided to put on a ball together. First they chose the venue, which was to be a large room above an inn. Then they organised the food and decorations. Lastly, they decided on the guest list.

‘What do you think of Jane Fairfax?’ asked Emma.

Frank thought for a moment. ‘I think she is quite dull,’ he replied. ‘And very plain. Don’t you agree?’

‘Frank!’ Emma said, shocked. She was also secretly pleased to hear something negative about Jane Fairfax for once.

‘I suppose we must invite her,’ Frank sighed. ‘I met her briefly a few months ago. I can’t avoid the connection.’

On the evening of the ball, Emma was delighted to see how well everything had turned out. She and Frank certainly worked well together. Emma had never been in love before and she couldn't help wondering if perhaps she was now.

I enjoy his company, she thought. Then, as she watched Frank adjusting his cravat, *He spends too much time on his appearance …*

Emma frowned. It was much easier making love matches for other people than for herself.

She was saved from thinking about the matter further when the first guests arrived. They were Miss Bates and Jane Fairfax.

Before Emma could greet them properly, Miss Bates began: 'Well now, Miss Woodhouse, what do you think has happened?' Emma opened her mouth to reply. 'You'll never guess, so I'll tell you. Jane has received the gift of a brand-new piano!'

'Goodness!' Emma looked at Jane. Jane did not look half as excited as Miss Bates. In fact, Jane looked quite uncomfortable. 'Who is the piano from?' Emma asked.

'That's the best part – *we don't know!*' Miss Bates clapped her hands together excitedly. 'Jane has so many admirers that it could be anyone. Although I do have one suspect in mind.' Here she leant closer to Emma, although she did not lower her voice. 'I have often seen Mr Knightley looking fondly at Jane.' Miss Bates giggled. 'Now if he would only propose, she wouldn't have to become a governess!'

Emma stood frozen, her stomach sinking. Mr Knightley? Would Mr Knightley really buy a piano for Jane Fairfax? It was true she had often heard him compliment Miss Fairfax's playing.

When Mr Knightley arrived, Emma wanted to take his arm and seat him next to her all evening. Right after she had pulled Miss Fairfax from her piano stool to keep her from playing any more. She was kept from either activity, however, by the arrival of Mr Elton – and his new wife.

Chapter 7

'May I introduce you to my wife, Miss Woodhouse,' said Mr Elton with a satisfied smile. 'Augusta and I met in Bath at Christmas, and she has made me the happiest of men.'

Emma forced her shocked face into a smile and curtseyed to the new Mrs Elton. She was sure

Harriet was nearby and wished she could warn her.

Mrs Elton looked around the room with a critical eye. 'What a small room,' she observed. 'And the decorations! Really, Miss Woodhouse, the next time there is a party you must consult me. I have excellent taste.'

'She certainly does,' replied Mr Elton. 'That's why she agreed to marry me!'

The awful pair laughed as they joined the rest of the ball.

Emma hurried to where Harriet and Jane Fairfax were sitting together. Harriet was already looking miserably at Mr and Mrs Elton.

'She is very fine,' said Harriet. 'She suits him better than I ever could have.'

'Only because you are too good for him!' said Emma.

Emma intended to stay and comfort her friend, when Frank Churchill suddenly appeared to ask Emma to dance. 'It is our ball after all,' he said, smiling and looking at

Jane for encouragement. 'What do you think, Miss Fairfax?'

'I am sure Miss Woodhouse can make up her own mind,' Jane mumbled.

As Emma danced, she felt the heaviness of the last half an hour lift. The idea of Mr Knightley buying a

piano for Jane. Meeting the ghastly Mrs Elton. It all seemed to evaporate with every step. Emma was having so much fun, that at first she didn't notice poor Harriet sitting alone. 'Oh dear,' she said, as the music started for another dance.

As Emma watched from the dance floor, Mrs Weston approached Harriet. 'My dear,' she said, 'we must find you a partner! Look, here is Mr Elton. Mr Elton, I have a fine dance partner for you here!'

Mr Elton looked at Harriet with a mixture of surprise and disgust. The memories of the night Emma Woodhouse had refused him came flooding back. To dance with a nobody like Harriet Smith, he felt, would be beneath him. 'I thank you,' he began, without a trace of gratitude. 'But I must return to *my wife*.'

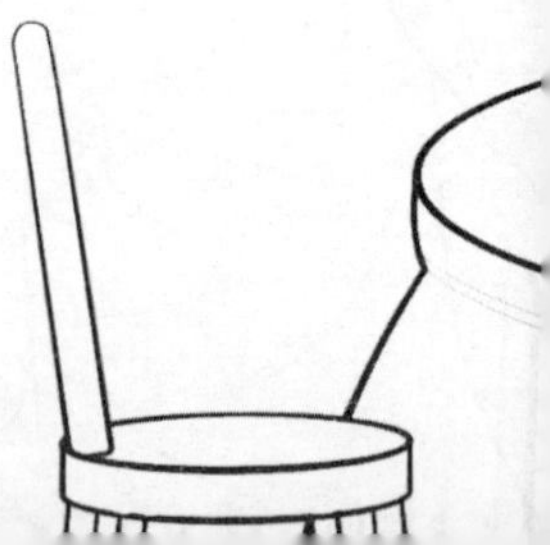

Harriet blushed and looked as if she was on the brink of crying. Emma's heart broke for her. She was about to excuse herself from the dance when a familiar figure appeared, clearly inviting Harriet to dance himself.

Mr Knightley! Emma beamed. *He really is the best of men.*

Chapter 8

The rest of the ball was a great success. The food was enjoyed (even by Mrs Elton, who ate a great deal despite complaining loudly that the dishes were very limited). Everyone danced, and even Jane Fairfax smiled once or twice.

So when Emma woke the following morning, she wondered why she felt so downhearted. Perhaps she was tired from all the dancing. Perhaps she was tired from listening to Miss Bates and Mrs Elton. One talked constantly about Jane Fairfax, the other about herself!

Or perhaps, Emma thought again, *I am in love?*

Emma's spirits only lifted when she saw that Mr Knightley had come to visit her father.

'Oh no, no, no,' Mr Woodhouse was saying as Emma entered the parlour. 'A picnic is a terrible idea this time of year! Think of the heat. Think of the cold. Think of the flies!'

‘A picnic? Who is going on a picnic?’ Emma asked, excitedly.

Mr Knightley stood, bowed to Emma and passed her a book he had been showing Mr Woodhouse.

‘I thought we could all go,’ he said. ‘To Box Hill. Everyone had such a nice time at the ball, our party could carry on here.’

Emma looked down at drawing of a hill with spectacular views. 'And who shall you invite?' Emma asked.

'Yourself, Mr Woodhouse–'

'Not me!' said Mr Woodhouse. 'And if Emma is to go, she must take a shawl!'

Emma smiled at Mr Knightley and urged him to continue.

'Miss Bates, Miss Fairfax, Miss Smith, the Westons and the Eltons–'

Emma rolled her eyes. 'The Eltons?'

'Yes!' Mr Knightley laughed. 'It would be impolite not to invite them … and of course, your Mr Churchill.'

'He's not *my* Mr Churchill,' Emma said quickly. 'And his aunt may want him to return home soon anyway.'

Mr Knightley looked at Emma for a moment longer than felt comfortable. 'I see,' he said. 'Ask him anyway. He's a lively fellow – he's sure to keep conversation flowing.'

As it happened, Frank Churchill's aunt was feeling unwell and told

Frank to stay a little longer with his father. Frank was in high spirits as he helped to load the picnic baskets onto the carriages at Donwell. The picnic party had agreed to set off from Mr Knightley's home and the weather was looking fine.

Harriet, Emma noticed, was wearing one of her best dresses. She stood near Mr Knightley's carriage until he asked her if she would like to ride to Box Hill with himself and Miss Bates.

Frank gently pulled Emma onto his own carriage and decided he would lead the way to Box Hill. Emma thought this a little rude as the picnic was Knightley's idea, but she shook the thought off. She was determined to enjoy herself today.

Chapter 9

Mr Woodhouse's worries proved correct. The picnic food was delicious and the view from the top of Box Hill was even more stunning than in Mr Knightley's book. However it was very hot, and the flies were enjoying the food almost as much as the guests.

‘Perhaps we should play a game!’ said Frank Churchill, jumping up from the picnic blanket.

‘What a good idea!’ said Mrs Elton. ‘My friends say that I am quite *brilliant* at games.’

‘We must all think of something to entertain Miss Woodhouse,’ said Frank, and Emma giggled.

Mrs Elton wasn’t used to playing games for the entertainment of someone else.

'I'm not sure I would be much good at entertaining Miss Woodhouse,' she sneered.

'In that case,' Frank began. 'We must all say one thing very clever, or two things moderately clever, or three things very dull indeed!'

The group all laughed at the plan.

The Eltons, however, declared that they were going for a walk instead.

'Well, I shall play,' said Miss Bates. 'I'm sure to say something dull as soon as I open my mouth!'

Emma laughed again. 'Ah, but there is the problem,' she said. 'How will you limit yourself to just three dull things?'

Emma thought her joke was rather clever. She couldn't understand why the rest of the group was looking at her so sternly – Mr Knightley especially.

'I see,' said Miss Bates quietly. 'I-I'm … sorry, I …'

To Emma's horror, Miss Bates's eyes were welling with tears. Before Emma could apologise, Mr Knightley offered to take Miss Bates for a walk too.

When the picnic had been cleared away, a rather quiet group of companions climbed back into their carriages. Emma wanted to leave as soon as possible, but Mr Knightley took her aside.

'Emma, how could you be so unfeeling towards Miss Bates?' In all the years she had known him,

Emma had not seen Mr Knightley so upset with her.

'I-I'm sure she didn't understand what I meant,' said Emma.

'I assure you she did. She has talked of nothing else. She is worried that you find her boring company. It was badly done, Emma. Badly done.'

Emma tried to apologise, but her breath got caught in her throat and she felt the hot sting of tears behind her eyes.

When the carriages arrived back at Donwell, Emma wanted nothing more than to walk alone back to Hartfield. Harriet had other plans.

‘Miss Woodhouse!’ she cried, skipping alongside her. ‘I must talk to you!’

Emma blinked away her tears and smiled at her friend. Harriet, at least, had not picked up on her meanness to Miss Bates.

‘What is it, Harriet?’ she asked.

‘I wanted to let you know that I have quite forgotten Mr Elton,’ she beamed. ‘In fact, I believe I might be in love with another.’

Emma was happy and relieved that her friend’s misery was over at last. ‘Oh Harriet! Who is the lucky fellow?’

‘Can’t you guess?’ said Harriet, laughing. ‘After he saved me at the ball?’

Emma searched her memory and stalled on one scene.

'I speak of Mr Knightley, of course!' said Harriet. 'When he took me onto the dance floor after Mr Elton snubbed me, I knew. *He* is the one.'

Chapter 10

If there had ever been a time when Emma was more unhappy, she could not remember it. The morning after the picnic, she visited Miss Bates with flowers from the Hartfield garden. She told Miss Bates how sorry she was for what she had said at the picnic. Miss Bates thanked her for the flowers and Emma knew she was forgiven, but she still felt guilty.

When she returned home, her

father told her that Mr Knightley had gone to London. Emma felt sure that he was avoiding her, and her unhappiness increased.

Emma spent the week quietly, avoiding Harriet and trying to make sense of the jumble of emotions she was feeling. Mainly she thought of Mr Knightley. She raged at the idea that he could be in love with Jane Fairfax and have bought her a piano. She despaired at the thought of Harriet falling in love with him, even as she understood it. He was so kind, so generous, so …

But did *he* like Harriet? He had asked her to dance, when he rarely danced. Then, when Emma had thanked him for that kindness, Mr Knightley even admitted that Harriet would have made a better wife for Mr Elton than the one he had chosen for himself.

As Emma returned from one of many walks in the Hartfield garden making sense of these thoughts, she was pleased to see Mrs Weston waiting for her.

'My dear, I have some news,' she said. Emma noticed the worried look on her face. 'I don't know how to tell you ...'

Emma immediately ran through the list of people she cared most for in the world. 'Is it Father? My sister? My nephews? Oh! Not Mr Knightley?'

Mrs Weston smiled. 'No, they are all fine. My news is about Frank. He is engaged to Jane Fairfax!'

Emma stepped back in shock. 'Jane Fairfax?!' she said, almost laughing at the idea. The two friends took a seat on a pretty bench facing the garden. Mrs Weston explained.

Two days ago, Frank's aunt, Mrs Churchill, had died. This meant that

her influence over Frank was over and he could now marry whoever he chose to. It seemed Frank and Jane had been secretly engaged since they met a few months earlier.

'He acted as though he didn't care for her!' Emma protested.

‘They had quarrelled,’ Mrs Weston explained. ‘Jane would not marry Frank if his aunt disapproved, and Frank was cross with her. It was he who bought the piano to say sorry. But Emma, are you sure you are all right?’

Emma looked at Mrs Weston and smiled. A smile more genuine than any that had crossed her face that week. 'Of course!' she replied. 'Frank's behaviour has been misleading and ungentlemanly, but I was never in love with him.'

For how could her heart have even been touched by a man like Frank Churchill, when it already belonged to a Mr Knightley?

Chapter 11

Emma waved goodbye to Mrs Weston, whose relief that Emma's heart was unbroken meant that she could now be truly happy about Frank's engagement. As Emma watched her friend walk down the lane that ran from Hartfield, she noticed Mr Knightley walking in the opposite direction.

Emma's heart pounded in her chest. She couldn't be sure if he was still angry at her about Miss Bates, or was perhaps coming to tell her that he was in love with someone else! In any case, she had no time to think of what to say.

'My dear Emma, I've heard the news about Jane Fairfax and Frank Churchill,' he began. 'And I am sorry for you.'

'You have no need to be,' she replied. 'I am happy for them. I never wished to be Frank Churchill's wife.'

‘I am relieved,’ said Mr Knightley. ‘Perhaps we could take a walk together. There is something I wish to tell you.’

Emma’s heart sank. Was this the moment he confessed his own disappointment over Frank and Miss Fairfax? Or declared his love for Harriet? Emma could not see any signs of heartbreak, but recent events had shown her that she did not understand people’s hearts as well as she had thought. Even her own.

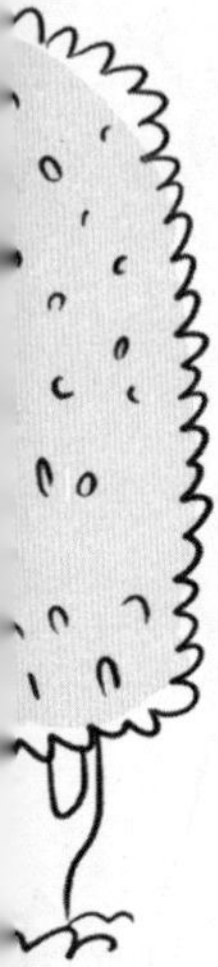

They walked slowly towards the rose garden.

'I am envious of Frank Churchill,' Mr Knightley began. 'Would you like to know why?'

No, Emma did not want to know why. However politeness kept her from saying so. 'I am your friend, Mr Knightley,' she said instead. 'I will hear anything you wish to tell me.'

'My friend? Then perhaps I shouldn't say any more.' Mr Knightley looked down. 'Yet I fear I must. Emma, have I no chance of winning your heart?'

Emma blinked. She looked at Mr Knightley to make sure she had heard him. For a moment she could not speak for the love she saw there.

'Emma, I am not one for great speeches,' Mr Knightley said. 'If I loved you less, I might be able to talk about it more. Instead I have lectured you and teased you and you have suffered it as no other woman would have. Emma, speak now and let me hear your answer.'

Emma was afraid the happiness might spring out of her. She flung her arms around Mr Knightley

and cried, 'Yes! Of course! *Yes!*'

As they broke from their embrace, however, Emma's face fell. 'Oh, but no, I can't! What about Harriet? And my father? I cannot leave him alone at Hartfield, and Harriet will be devastated.'

'Harriet Smith?' enquired Mr Knightley, and Emma explained Harriet's feelings for him. Mr Knightley did not look concerned when she had finished, only even happier, if that were possible.

He took Emma's trembling hand. 'My love, yesterday I received a letter from Robert Martin. He wanted my permission to marry – to marry Miss Harriet Smith. She has accepted him this time.'

Emma gasped. 'Are you certain?'

'Quite certain,' he replied. 'As to your fears about leaving your father, I am perfectly happy to move to Hartfield to be with you both.'

Emma felt as though her heart would burst. It was like a dream! And best of all, everyone else seemed happy, too.

In the following months, a flurry of weddings took place at Highgate. Mr Elton had never been so busy! First, Frank Churchill and Jane Fairfax were married. They had been a secret for so long, they could not wait to make their union official.

The next couple was Robert Martin and Harriet Smith. Emma was pleased to attend. She could see that she had been wrong to persuade her friend against him all those months ago.

Finally, Emma and Mr Knightley were married in front of all their friends and relations. Then, as the story goes, they lived happily ever after.